D0575883

THE ESSENTIAL GUIDE

Written by Jo Casey

CONTENTS

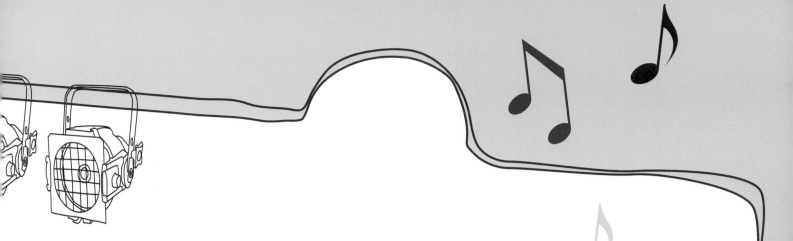

INTRODUCTION

Meet JONAS. Kevin, Joe, and Nick Lucas are three brothers, living the rock star dream. When they're not writing the next JONAS smash hit or performing for their fans, Kevin, Joe, and Nick are trying to lead ordinary lives. They go to school, hang out with their friends, and do their chores—which is not so easy while being followed by their fans! It's a crazy life but the boys have learned that if you work hard and believe in your dreams, anything is possible. Read on to discover more about the rockin' world of JONAS....

MEET THE BAND

Rockin' out on stage night after night in packed stadiums and playing music that rocks the stage, is what JONAS is all about. Kevin, Joe, and Nick each have different talents—Kevin is into guitars, Joe has a stunning singing voice, and Nick writes smash hit songs, but together, they make the unique JONAS sound. They are a rock sensation!

Kevin

DID YOU KNOW?
Kevin's favorite part about touring (apart from the fans) is staying in hotels. He loves the tiny shampoo bottles!

"FRIENDS AND FAMILY COME FIRST."

Joe

Nick

KEVIN LUCAS

Kevin is the eldest Lucas and is known as "The Peacemaker" within the band. His witty one-liners and quirky humor can always be relied on to lighten the mood if things ever get a little too intense.

DID YOU KNOW?
Kevin once played Elvis Presley in the school talent show.

Rockin' Out

One guitar isn't enough for Kevin—he's obsessed with them and stores hundreds on a revolving dry-cleaning rack in his room. He even has his own "Kevin-ated" guitar with a neck that stretches three times the length of a normal guitar.

If the boys need to say it with a card, they turn to Kevin. He has a greeting card for every occasion in his locker. From "Happy Belated Wednesday" to "Congratulations on your New Nose", Kevin has it covered.

KEVIN LUCAS FACTFILE

NICKNAME: "The Peacemaker"

LIKES: Guitars, sideburns, drinking tea from a china teacup, Nick's homemade cookies

DISLIKES: Being sensible, bees (he's allergic to them)

Kind Kevin doesn't like being mean and has an inability to lie. So when Stella makes him a sweater, he just can't tell her that he hates it!

Health Kick

Smoothies are ideal for getting that extra immunity boost. Kevin even has a smoothie maker in his locker!

Cool cravat smartens up any look.

Kevin doesn't shy away from flowery prints.

"GUYS, CHECK OUT MY NEW GUITAR!"

Eccentric Style

Kevin isn't afraid to push the fashion boundaries. From preppy cool to rock star chic, Kevin can work any look (with a little help from JONAS stylist, Stella.)

Just one of Kevin's many guitars.

The band has a hectic schedule but Joe always makes sure he finds time to chill.

He likes to think of himself as just a regular Joe, but sometimes Joe Lucas has his face on the cover of teen magazines! A bit of a daydreamer, Joe is always thinking up sensational stunts for the next JONAS concert—they don't call him "Danger" for nothing!

Fashion Victim

Joe causes a fashion emergency by getting an ink stain on the shirts Stella made for JONAS' meeting with the Prime Minister of England. Later, her payback comes in the form of an OTT costume that does nothing for Joe's rock star reputation!

Making the cover of a magazine comes with the territory of being a rock star—Joe wouldn't mind but in this case, he's not exactly rockin' the JONAS signature style in Stella's payback costume!

Pen Please!

Having their house surrounded by JONAS fans does have its bonuses. If the boys ever need a pen, or even a hundred of them, they just need to ask!

JOE LUCAS FACTFILE

NICKNAME: "Danger"

LIKES: Doing cartwheels on stage, slick hair, panda bears, sunglasses

DISLIKES: Upsetting Stella, bad hair days

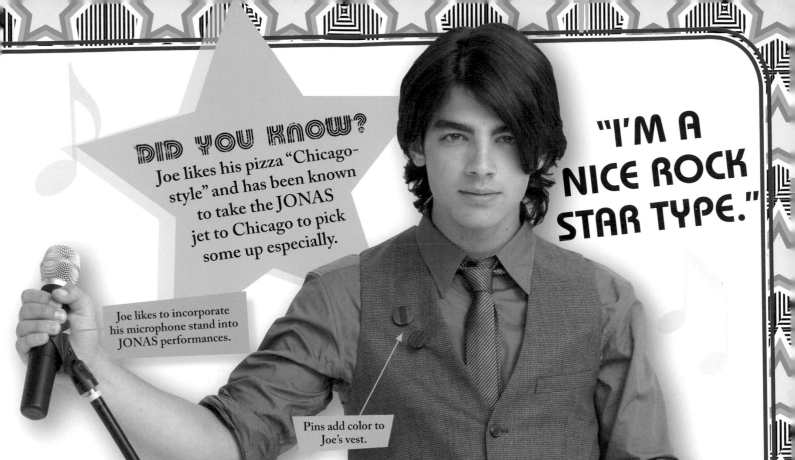

DID YOU KNOW?
Joe likes his pizza "Chicago-style" and has been known to take the JONAS jet to Chicago to pick some up especially.

Joe likes to incorporate his microphone stand into JONAS performances.

Pins add color to Joe's vest.

Beads give Joe's look a rock star edge.

Joe's talent for the triangle impresses everyone at the school recital. Kevin and Nick also step in to rework classical pieces, JONAS-style.

Daredevil

When it comes to performing, Joe's style is anything but regular. He always adds his own signature moves to give JONAS fans a performance to remember—and his Mom, Sandy, an anxiety attack!

NICK LUCAS

Nick takes his responsibilities in the band very seriously, and his intensity means he always writes really cool songs. A natural-born leader, Nick always makes sure the band gets in enough practice before hitting the stage. His brothers call him "Mr. President." If he can keep Kevin and Joe under control who says he can't lead the country one day!

Trademark curly hair.

Extra Moist

Let's Bake!

For their Mom's birthday, Kevin decides to surprise her with a cake. But Kevin and Joe don't even know what a colander is, so it's a good thing that Nick started cooking at the tender age of five.

Mega Musicality

Nick's talent for music is obvious. Underneath his calm exterior is a passion for all things musical that is unleashed as soon as he steps on stage. Whether he's playing punk or Prokofiev, his musicianship is off the scale!

Orange t-shirt

The guitar is just one of the many instruments Nick can play.

Regular Wordsmith

Nick is a whiz when it comes to words and he is always thinking up new rockin' JONAS lyrics. As soon as they return from their concert tour, Nick gets straight to work on the next album. His biggest worry is writer's block, but inspiration can strike anywhere—even in the shower!

If Nick is ever struggling with a tricky lyric, he knows that he can always turn to Kevin and Joe to lighten his mood and offer up some sound brotherly advice.

DID YOU KNOW?

Nick won a second place ribbon for his banana bread when he was eleven years old.

NICK LUCAS FACTFILE

NICKNAME: "Mr. President"

LIKES: Cooking, touring, nachos, songwriting

DISLIKES: Writer's block

Listen Up!

He might be the youngest member of JONAS, but Nick is never afraid to speak up and voice his opinion—when he talks, Kevin and Joe always listen!

"I HOPE I DON'T HAVE WRITER'S BLOCK."

FRANKIE LUCAS

Frankie Lucas might only be eight years old and four feet tall, but he makes sure he gets his voice heard over the sound of guitars and drums at the firehouse. He also gets his fair share of rock star perks—his school transport is the JONAS limousine!

Rock Star in Training

Frankie likes to think of himself as the fourth member of JONAS. With his fedora hat and bow tie, he has the JONAS look down. Well, he has learned from the best!

When Kevin, Nick, and Joe return home from their concert tour, Frankie is happy to have his brothers back.

Sandy is happiest surrounded by all her boys.

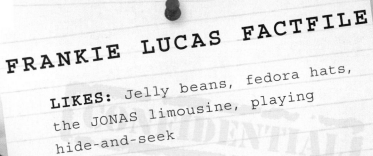

FRANKIE LUCAS FACTFILE

LIKES: Jelly beans, fedora hats, the JONAS limousine, playing hide-and-seek

DISLIKES: Green jelly beans

"I'LL BE IN MY MAN-CAVE."

Frankie's favorite game to play with his brothers is hide-and-seek. He can remain hidden for days—as long as he has a big jar of jelly beans to keep him going!

Frankie has the same sweet smile as his brothers.

DID YOU KNOW?
Frankie has a bear named "Frankie-Bear." Sometimes they even dress the same!

17

No rock band would be complete without a stylist. JONAS have their own style guru, Stella Malone, to thank for their rock star look. Whether she's creating a new line of "fan-proof" clothing or sketching the latest fashion-forward look, Stella never loses her cool. She has just one rule—no clashing allowed!

When it comes to fashion, Stella doesn't follow the crowd, they follow her. She carries her sketchpad with her everywhere she goes.

After one too many of her JONAS designs are ruined by fans tearing the boys clothes, Stella creates a new line of clothing called "Stelcroe." Now, when fans grab JONAS' jackets, only the sleeve breaks away—so less work for Stella!

DID YOU KNOW?

Stella can text on four cell phones at the same time using her hands and feet!

Best Friends

Stella and Macy might have totally different interests—style and soccer—but they are still the closest of pals. And they do have one major thing in common—JONAS!

Joe and Stella's elaborate handshake involves their pinkies, elbows, knees, and hips. It always eases any tension that Stella's no-nonsense attitude to fashion sometimes causes.

A Friend in Need

Stella has known the boys since they were kids and is part of the Lucas family. She's willing to sacrifice fashion for friends to help the boys recreate home movies for their Mom's birthday.

"YOU HAVE TO LOOK AMAZING!"

Stella wears pretty accessories to give her uniform a unique twist.

Stella customizes her uniform, but always abides by the school rules.

Stylish Stella

Stella is always on call to ensure Kevin, Joe, and Nick stand out from the HMA crowd and she custom-makes their uniforms especially. Any changes the boys want to make to their look have to be approved by her—after all, she has a reputation as a trendsetter to uphold!

Stella believes that no phone equals no life. But when Stella bets Macy that she can go longer without texting on her cell phone than she can go without mentioning JONAS, both their willpower is put to the test.

Chunky boots give Stella's look a funky edge.

MACY

Macy Misa is the star athlete at Horace Mantis Academy. She's always carrying some kind of sporting equipment, which makes her a hallway hazard! She is also a mega JONAS fan—when she's not thinking about JONAS she's talking about JONAS or following JONAS. She still can't believe they attend HMA...not that she could actually talk to them or anything!

Macy wears her uniform with pride.

Plaid skirt in the HMA colors.

There's no doubt that Macy is JONAS' No.1 fan. She always carries a binder that opens up to reveal a 3-D pop-up of JONAS on stage and she's even working on a JONAS mosaic!

Sports Star

Away from the sports field Macy is sensitive and sweet, but as soon as she changes into her sports gear, she reveals a whole other aggressive side to her personality!

Macy's dream is to be a pro singer so when the JONAS back-up singer cancels, the boys decide to make her dream come true. However, her singing is so bad, it causes Kevin to faint! But Macy enjoys singing so much, she makes the time to belt out some tunes in the atrium.

From football to field hockey and bowling to basketball, there's no sport that Macy can't master. She's even the leading basketball scorer in the state!

"I WAS JUST WORKING ON A NEW SERVE."

On the sports field Macy is as graceful as a dancer but away from it she turns into a mighty klutz. Being near JONAS only makes it worse. They've learned that it's best to keep a safe distance from Macy in the hallway!

DID YOU KNOW?
Macy sometimes works in her Mom's vintage store.

Ms. President
Macy is President of the JONAS fan club and takes her role very seriously. But when it comes to getting exclusive interviews with the boys, Macy gets so nervous she shakes, stammers, and swallows her gum!

Sleeve Souvenir
Stella is less than impressed when Macy confesses to ripping Nick's shirt sleeve off at a JONAS concert—she ruined a perfectly good shirt!

TOM LUCAS

Tom Lucas is not only the boys' dad, he is also the manager of JONAS. From working out the technicalities of a JONAS concert to monitoring Joe's dangerous stunts, he likes to think of himself as the grease that keeps the JONAS machine running smoothly.

DID YOU KNOW?
Tom once caught the foul ball at Yankee Stadium.

The Dadager

Having their Dad as the manager of JONAS is definitely a bonus—they get to spend lots of quality time together. Whether Tom is in "manager mode" or "Dad mode", he is always ready to offer up sound advice to his boys.

Wearing leprechaun hats is a must when watching "Leprechaun Hunter."

Donning a hat and watching "Leprechaun Hunter" on TV is the perfect way to chill after a busy day managing JONAS.

Near-identical remote controls can cause confusion!

JONAS Promotion

As JONAS' manager, Tom is always on a "merch search" for the next big thing in JONAS merchandise. He is the proud owner of JONAS slippers, bathrobe, and shower cap. He has even found a JONAS boomerang and JONAS jerky!

"WHY IS THERE SHEET MUSIC IN THE SHOWER?"

Smart suit for attending business meetings in.

When the boys order pizza from the worst pizza place in town to get close to the cute delivery girl, Tom finds himself chewing cheese for a long time!

When Sandy starts calling Joe "Joseph", the boys know that they are in trouble!

SANDY LUCAS

Being the parent of rock stars is not always easy, but Sandy Lucas works hard to make sure her boys stay grounded and don't get too big for their rock star boots. Just because they are famous doesn't mean they don't have to do their chores! But no matter how successful Kevin, Joe, and Nick get, they are never too famous to spend some time with their Mom.

Memory Lane

Sandy can't believe how quickly her boys are growing up. Watching home movies brings back great memories from the past, but she wouldn't change the present for anything!

Sandy is the proudest Mom in the world. As long as her family are safe, healthy, and together, she is always smiling.

Mom Alert

For Sandy, family always comes first. But when band meetings start interrupting normal family life, Sandy uses her special "Do your chores" look to give Kevin, Joe, and Nick a reality check—by getting them to take out the trash!

Mom is JONAS' No.1 fan (apart from Macy!)

"I'M SO PROUD OF YOU GUYS."

DID YOU KNOW?
Sandy regularly goes to garage sales, searching for old fire helmets to add to her collection.

BIG ROB

Wherever JONAS go, their burly bodyguard Big Rob goes too. He always keeps the band safe—nothing gets past this human brick wall! Big Rob might look scary, but he has a big heart and is treated just like a member of the Lucas family.

Big Rob is really big!

Diet Police

Big Rob doesn't only keep an eye on JONAS fans, he also carefully monitors Kevin, Nick, and Joe's diets. There is no junk food allowed with Big Rob around. And they don't disobey Big Rob, because, well, he's so big!

Rock star bling

DID YOU KNOW?

Big Rob regularly takes Frankie to school in the JONAS limousine.

BIG ROB FACTFILE

NICKNAME: "The Big Man"

LIKES: Quiet JONAS fans, helping Frankie with his homework

DISLIKES: JONAS fans tearing his clothes

"I'M NOT LEAVING YOUR SIDE."

Blending In

Meeting the Queen of England is a big deal for JONAS—and that calls for big security! It might seem impossible for such a huge guy to blend into the background, but Rob's talents as a bodyguard ensure that the spotlight stays firmly on JONAS.

Security Please!

It's always reassuring for the boys to know that the Big Man is around on a big night out. Kevin, Nick, Joe, and their pals can have a great night out, safe in the knowledge that Big Rob will always watch their backs.

Big Rob is on high alert.

JONAS STREET

Kevin's colorful collection of guitars is his most prized possession. They take pride of place on his dry cleaning rack.

There is nothing quite like returning home from a concert tour or busy day at school. And there's no place like the Lucas family home—it's a converted firehouse! Located on Jonas Street, the firehouse is where the Lucas family work together and play together. It has everything a rock star family could ever need, all under one roof.

Who Needs Stairs?

A firehouse just wouldn't be a firehouse without a firepole, and this one has three—one each for Kevin, Joe, and Nick. If an emergency band meeting is called or the boys just need to make a quick exit, taking the poles is definitely way more rock star than taking the stairs!

"AHH. IT'S GOOD TO BE HOME."

Breakfast at the firehouse is the perfect time for Tom to catch up with his boys before the busy day ahead. It's also the time when Joe most likes to play with his remote control toys!

Making music is thirsty work! Stocking up on healthy snacks and scrumptious smoothies from the juice bar ensures the boys are always at the top of their game.

JONAS' creative juices are always flowing and they don't like to go too long without making music. Luckily, they have a mini recording studio to experiment with new sounds.

Brass firepoles

Recording booth

There's no taking the stairs for these rock stars!

DID YOU KNOW?
When they were kids, Kevin, Joe, and Nick fought over a teddy bear named Mr. Bumble.

Home Sweet Home
Music inspired the decor of the firehouse, but it's first and foremost a family home. Sandy and Tom's special touches, like cozy rugs and comfy sofas, make the firehouse a heartwarming home for the whole family.

Pumping Iron
Performing on stage takes a lot of energy, so the boys have to put in the hours at their gym to keep in shape. Joe also makes the time to give his fingers a workout, by flicking through a magazine!

THE LOFT

When the JONAS boys need some time-out from their busy schedule, they can usually be found lounging in The Loft. It has lots of rock star features so the boys never get bored. But if they miss the bright lights too much, they can always practice their rock star moves on the stage!

You've Got Mail!

The Loft is the perfect place for Joe to slip on his slippers and surround himself with JONAS fan mail. Reading inspiring letters from fans makes all of their hard work worthwhile.

DID YOU KNOW?
Nick has won lots of songwriting awards. In first grade he won "Best Melody in an Original Alphabet Song."

Forty Winks

Kevin loves being on the road touring so much that he has his very own tour bus bunk bed in The Loft. He finds it impossible to switch off unless his traffic sounds and flashing headlights are switched on!

The Loft is where Kevin, Nick, and Joe come up with ideas for new songs, discuss the latest gossip at school, or just chill with a magazine.

"OOPS. THAT ACTIVATES THE CONFETTI."

Boys' Toys

It's gadgets galore at The Loft—a popcorn machine, foosball table, giant TV, and even a confetti machine, all help to keep the boys amused. But when they can't tell the "drum-lower-er" control from the TV control, Kevin gets the bright idea to make a remote with a broom and a rubber hand—problem solved!

Lounge chairs for lounging on.

A broom isn't just for sweeping!

LIVING THE DREAM

Living the dream can mean a lot of different things. For Kevin, Nick, and Joe, being in a rock band is a dream come true. They get to make the music they love with the people they love! The boys know that life is no rehearsal, and they intend to make the most of it. JONAS really are living their dream!

JONAS are all about great teamwork. They know exactly how to bring out the best in each other.

Rock Royalty

JONAS often do benefit concerts—it's their way of giving something back to their fans. But they get a royal shock when a meeting with the Prime Minister of England turns out to be a meeting with the *Queen* of England! She presents JONAS with Commendations of Merit for all their good work.

Attending glamourous parties is just one of the fabulous perks of being a rock star. And as pals of JONAS, Stella and Macy sometimes get to experience them too!

DID YOU KNOW?

Inside the JONAS limousine is a hot tub, trampoline, yogurt machine, and automatic massage seat!

"WE'VE GOT SOME VERY ENTHUSIASTIC FANS."

Music Matters

Sharing their love for music is what matters most to Kevin, Joe, and Nick. They are always involved in every aspect of the music-making process—from writing the melody, laying down the vocals, and working in the recording studio, they make sure every track is pure JONAS!

Charmed Life

Living the rock star life is anything but boring. JONAS could be performing on stage one day, and recording vocals the next—every day is different! But whatever the boys are doing, they always turn on the JONAS charm.

THE FAME GAME

Rock and roll superstardom isn't all glitz and glamour—the JONAS boys have to put in a lot of hard work, too. Combining student life with the rock star life often means late nights and early starts. But Kevin, Joe, and Nick wouldn't change a thing—performing or studying, JONAS always rock it!

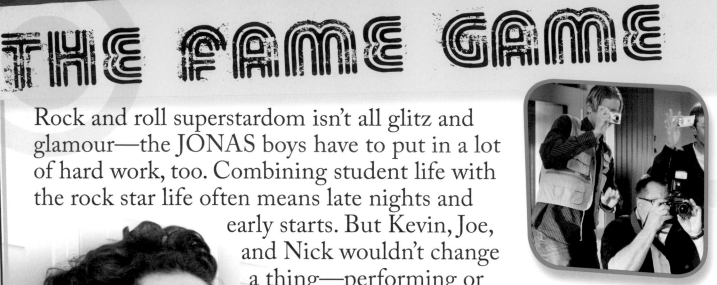

Wherever JONAS go, the paparazzi always follow.

Shades to block out bright lights.

What City Are We In?

Slacking off at school is not an option for the boys. They know that studying is just as important as singing. But touring non-stop for ten weeks takes its toll and a power nap before class starts is sometimes necessary!

Fan Magnets

The boys cause a media frenzy wherever they go. But at school, the JONAS boys can pretty much cruise the hallways without any hassle. Except, that is, when a choir visit—they go crazy for JONAS. But the boys always treat their fans with respect. Except when they are running in the opposite direction!

DID YOU KNOW?
Kevin has a lucky charm—a boot, which he wears playing JONAS concerts.

"I'VE GOT TO FINISH OFF THESE SONGS FOR THE NEXT ALBUM."

Being in a rock band takes dedication, and JONAS have lots of it. The boys never shy away from hard work, and always put in the extra hours. Practicing on weekends and all-night rehearsals are just what it takes to be the best!

SCHOOL ROCKS!

Welcome to Horace Mantis Academy! The school spirit at HMA is all about working hard, but also making time for fun. Extracurricular activities are taken very seriously at HMA, and there is something for everyone to really rock at!

Unique Uniforms

Wearing a uniform doesn't have to mean blending in. The students find their own unique ways of standing out from the HMA crowd. Stella uses ace accessories in the HMA colors, while Macy sticks to what she knows best— sports gear!

Standing out

De-ten-shuun!

Vice Principal Smetzer is super-strict and very particular about students following school rules. Even walking on the grass can lead to detention.

36

Lunchtime

The cafeteria isn't just a place to have lunch. It's the place where students catch up on all the hot topics of the day—who is voting for whom for class President and who got what score in the biology test. Sometimes, they're even treated to an impromptu performance.

Lunchtime is fun time!

Orchestra Club

The Orchestra Club is the perfect place for all the musical maestros at HMA to showcase their talent on the triangle or skills on the cymbal.

Go team!

From archery to lacrosse, at HMA there is a sport for everyone to shine at. And with Mighty Mite Macy Misa on their side, HMA is rarely the losing team!

FRIENDSHIP

JONAS might have busy schedules but nothing ever gets in the way of Kevin, Joe, and Nick spending quality time with their best buddies. Their fame might not last forever, but they know that their friendships always will.

Stella takes best pal Macy's love for all things JONAS in her stride. Her collection of "JONAS-abilia" (something the boys have touched, used, or worn), like the "Joe-Tato" chip, is just what makes Macy so unique!

Stella is much more than a stylist to the JONAS boys. She's a super friend too!

When Nick suffers a rare bout of writer's block, his bros are right by his side, urging him to be inspired. They are even willing to give him a foot rub—now that's brotherly love!

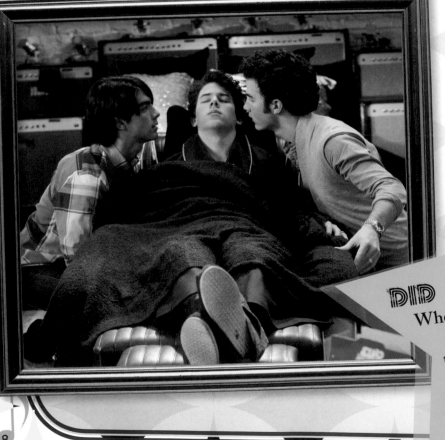

DID YOU KNOW?
When Macy broke her leg, Stella painted her toenails so they would look pretty when people signed her cast.

JONAS can always rely on best pal Stella to get them out of a crisis. Dressing them in disguises saves them from being ambushed by their fans...and gives Kevin an idea for a second career—as a sailor!

When old pal Carl Schuster ruins Kevin's guitar, he doesn't mind too much. He knows that guitars can be replaced, good friends can't.

"WE'VE GOT A REALLY TIGHT FRIENDSHIP."

Hug it Out

Kevin, Joe, and Nick might get competitive playing Hacky Sack, but JONAS are all about great teamwork. They have an unbreakable bond that makes them awesome bandmates and brilliant best friends. Nothing comes between them—not even a Hacky Sack!

Stella just can't bring herself to try her hand at handstands—she's lousy at all sports! But Macy helps Stella realize that she has her own special talents. Anybody who says she's not an athlete hasn't seen her with a pair of scissors and a measuring tape!

THE STELLAVATOR

Stella is so passionate about fashion she has a wardrobe named after her! But her invention, The Stellavator, is no ordinary wardrobe. Whatever outfit the boys want is just typed on to the touchpad screen, and the mechanical rack brings the exact same outfit out of the wardrobe. The boys are transformed from preppy students to rock star-ready, all in the touch of a button!

The same co-ordinated outfit on the touchpad screen slides out on the clothing rack.

Techno Fashion

Stella is not only super-stylish, she's also super-organized. Every piece of clothing in The Stellavator is cross-referenced by brother, season, occasion, and fashion-curve, which, thanks to Stella, the boys are ahead of.

Stella has tailored Kevin's look to suit his sophisticated tastes. Luxurious fabrics and hip hats reflect his fun, quirky personality.

Velvet blazer adds a touch of class

"WE HAVE A FASHION EMERGENCY!"

Kevin's favorite accessory is his guitar

A vest is always a winner

Nick looks every inch the perfect student!

Nick is pretty laid back when it comes to fashion and is most comfortable working the casual-cool look. He prefers his sleeves rolled up, because he is always ready to get down to some hard work!

Casual-chic

Touchpad screen

Tie smartens up tux

DID YOU KNOW?
Stella custom-makes Kevin, Nick, and Joe's school uniforms.

Cool shades for a cool dude

Joe knows how to work a tux!

Slick shades and bright bow ties transform Joe from smooth student to rockin' rock star!

Smart daytime look

A JONAS concert is always an ambitious production, full of show-stopping special effects and cutting-edge technology. With a little help from their rock-star gear, JONAS never fail to entertain!

Unique Talent

It takes a lot of gear to achieve the unique JONAS sound. But it's the boys' talent that really counts—and this trio have tons of it!

Kevin is in-tune with all his guitars. The hardest part about going on tour is deciding which ones to take!

Electric guitars contribute to the unique JONAS sound.

Feel the Beat

JONAS make playing the drums look easy. But it takes skill, concentration, and lots of rockin' rhythm to master this instrument!

Joe's stunts are legendary. Sometimes he even does fantastic flips off the amps!

"YOU GUYS SOUND AWESOME."

JONAS' precious guitars are packed away in cases to protect them from bumps and scratches when being transported from venue to venue.

Joe uses the microphone stand to show off his dance moves.

Large speakers

Guitar amp

DID YOU KNOW?
Kevin loves his guitars so much, he has given them names! A few of his favorites are called Lulu, Olivia, and Grace.

SEE INSIDE FOR YOUR CHANCE TO WIN THE BRILLIANT BOA

The New Ji

New Jersey's No.1 newspaper with

$1.00

JONAS T
ON, SAY

Star pupil Nick attends HMA

We believed in him, say pals

BY A.J. FAN

Nick Lucas, the youngest member of JONAS, is known for his sensational songwriting skills and dedication to his studies at Horace Mantis Academy. Close friends of the band

rsey Times

r 2.5 million readers everyday!

No. 3001

FULL STORY: PAGES 3 & 4

OUR IS BACK BROTHERS

BY JO CASEY

It has been a case of on-again, off-again, but *The New Jersey Times* **can exclusively reveal that JONAS' much anticipated "Bigger and Better than the Last Tour" tour is officially back on again.**

Nick Lucas and his brothers and bandmates, Kevin and Joe, had to pass their exams so that they would be free to launch the tour. However, millions of JONAS fans around the world were left heartbroken yesterday with the shocking news that Nick, JONAS' songwriter, had failed his geometry exam. But JONAS, renowned for their teamspirit, weren't going to let a few geometry laws come between them and a world tour. So they did what they do best. They wrote a song using all the geometry laws and performed them with Nick so that he would remember them. Reports that a geometry song will be on the next album have yet to be confirmed.

KEEPING IT REAL

JONAS are all about keeping it real. Despite all of their success and commitments, offstage, Kevin, Joe, and Nick try and lead as ordinary a life as possible. Whatever happens, there is always room in the JONAS schedule for some Lucas family time!

The JONAS boys know that their pals help them to keep it real. To show Stella how much she means to them all, Joe even throws her a surprise party to celebrate their fifteen-year "Friend-A-Versary."

DID YOU KNOW?
Kevin's favorite breakfast is guitar-shaped pancakes.

"WE PROMISE TO KEEP IT REAL."

Ambush!

Keeping it real is sometimes harder than it looks. Doing a simple chore for Mom, like taking their old clothes to the thrift store, causes a JONAS fan frenzy.

When the boys accidentally destroy their Mom's home movies, they decide to recreate moments from their childhood. They would do anything to make their Mom happy—even if it involves wearing a handlebar mustache!

Team JONAS

The success of JONAS is all down to great teamwork. Having their family around them helps the JONAS boys stay grounded. They all work together at keeping it real— go team JONAS!

LONDON, NEW YORK, MELBOURNE,
MUNICH, AND DELHI

Senior Designer Lisa Sodeau
Editor Jo Casey
Managing Editor Catherine Saunders
Art Director Lisa Lanzarini
Publishing Manager Simon Beecroft
Category Publisher Alex Allan
Production Editor Sean Daly
Print Production Nick Seston

First published in the United States in 2009
by DK Publishing
375 Hudson Street
New York, New York 10014

09 10 11 12 13 10 9 8 7 6 5 4 3 2 1
DD537—07/09

Based on the series created by Michael Curtis
& Roger S.H. Schulman

Copyright © 2009 Disney Enterprises, Inc.
Page design copyright © 2009 DK Publishing, Inc.
The publisher would like to thank Steve Gorton, Dave King, Howard
Shooter, and Tim Ridley © Dorling Kindersley for kind permission to
reproduce the photographs on pages 36, 37, and 39.

All rights reserved under International and Pan-American
Copyright Conventions. No part of this publication may be
reproduced, stored in a retrieval system, or transmitted in
any form or by any means, electronic, mechanical,
photocopying, recording, or otherwise, without the prior
written permission of the copyright owner.
Published in Great Britain by
Dorling Kindersley Limited.

DK books are available at special discounts when
purchased in bulk for sales promotions, premiums,
fundraising, or educational use. For details, contact:
DK Publishing Special Markets
375 Hudson Street
New York, New York 10014
SpecialSales@dk.com

A catalog record for this book is available from the
Library of Congress.

ISBN: 978-0-7566-5516-7

Color reproduction by MDP, in the UK
Printed and bound in the USA by Lake Book Mfg.

Discover more at
www.dk.com

Kevin

Joe

Nick